Grandma's Scrapbook

BY JOSEPHINE NOBISSO

ILLUSTRATED BY
MAUREEN HYDE

Gingerbread House
Westhampton Beach, New York

Gingerbread House
602 Montauk Highway
Westhampton Beach
New York 11978

1 (631) 288-5119
Fax 1 (631) 288-5179
e-mail: ghbooks@optonline.net
www.gingerbreadbooks.com

Original version published by The Green Tiger Press
Subsequently published by Simon & Schuster
Gingerbread House SAN: 217-0760

3 1759 50042 0959

Printed in Hong Kong
Manufactured by Regent Publishing Services Ltd.

Revised 2000
10 9 8 7 6 5 4 3 2 1

Publisher's Cataloging-in-Publication *(Provided by Quality Books, Inc.)*
Nobisso, Josephine.
 Grandma's scrapbook / by Josephine Nobisso;
 illustrated by Maureen Hyde. – 2nd ed.
  p. cm.
  SUMMARY: A scrapbook provides many memories of
 good times enjoyed with Grandma.
  LCCN: 99-75394
  ISBN: 0-940112-02-7

  1. Grandmothers—Juvenile fiction.
2. Scrapbooks--Juvenile fiction. 3. Grandmothers--Death--Juvenile fiction.
4. Grief in children--Juvenile fiction. 5. Bereavement in children--Juvenile fiction.
I. Hyde, Maureen, ill. II. Title.

PZ7.N6645Gr 2000   [E]
          QBI99-1373

*For my mother Mary (Maria) Zamboli Nobisso who, at the age of 65,
stopped a Long Island Railroad train with the power of her love and devotion.
And for her four granddaughters, Nicolle, Gina, Bianca and Maria.*
                                                                    --J.N.

To Mary and Elise, with special thanks to Ali, Shana and Louise.
                                                                    --M.H.

Grandma's hair was once black as crows. I was too young to remember, but I know it was so because Grandma kept a scrapbook.

*The first pages are of me as a baby— looking
dopey before I fall asleep, and silly as I yawn, and
like a monkey with ears so big, and coconut-head so bald.
Here's a tiny envelope with wisps of baby hair in it, and
beside it, a braided lock of Grandma's hair, black as crows.*

*H*ere I am in my stroller. Grandma used to push me through the garden. I would grab at the flowers as we passed, until Grandma managed to teach me to snip one just right.

She saved that faded flower, pressing it between the pages of the scrapbook.

I 'm older in these. Just looking brings back the smell of salt air in her back yard, and of crushed grass, and of fishy bay mud on Bella's paws. I can hear the frogs and the crickets, and the water lapping against the shore.

From the dock, we watched red evenings turn to black nights. Then Grandma would call every star she knew by name. The next thing I knew, it was morning, and I was under my quilt in my room at Grandma's. She'd carry me in all by herself.

In the scrapbook she saved a seashell I'd once clasped in my hand.

Here we are another year, in bathing suits and hats– me all arms and legs, and Grandma a natural beauty. We were having cocoa in fancy chipped cups, being proper and very giddy.

*S*he rode me on the back of her bicycle, and in
the village we bought a picnic lunch.

"How far to the ocean?" I asked.

"Half a mile as the crow flies," Grandma told me.
She peddled to the edge of a field, and we watched the
bright blue skies for a crow. A seagull flapped by instead.
Grandma shrugged and laughed. "It's not a crow, but it
will know the way!"

She followed it, swerving to avoid the gopher holes.
Then the bird turned and flew the other way. "Hey!"
Grandma called, laughing and shaking her fist at the sky.
"Where are you taking us?"

*B*ut already I could hear the waves, roaring as they broke and sighing as they slid back into the sea. And already I could see the bridge. "That way! That way, Grandma!" I cried.

At each wave, Grandma lifted me over her head, taking a dunking herself. She sputtered as she came up, and I squealed the next warning: "A wave! A wave!" so that she could bob and dance with the ocean's rolls. "A wave!" I called to the gulls.

She took me shopping. I picked funny face mugs for my parents, a "Maw" and a "Paw". I got a reflecting heart for Bella's collar, and a sparkling ring bigger than an acorn for Grandma.

That was the year she bought me my own camera. We took nutty shots of each other, and this one of Bella wearing my sunglasses. Then we rode the dirt paths home through the woods, breaking their silence with our cackling.

When it cooled in the evenings, we picked garden greens for dinner and flowers for the table. Sometimes Grandma's friends came, and we all howled songs around the piano.

She'd send everyone home early– "Because there's a child in the house!" And sometimes she'd take out the scrapbook. "What times we've had!" I told her.

"Yes," she agreed, "every year we change and grow." And the scrapbook was making everything more precious, as though without it, some of our memories would be lost.

*A*t night Grandma read to me from my favorite books on her shelves. Sometimes I fell asleep dreaming about the rolling, rushing sea. A wave! A wave!

My parents couldn't come to pick me up one year, and I wanted to ride the train alone. "I've grown big enough!" I told Grandma.

"I believe you have!" she agreed.

When it was time to say good-bye, the sting from my sun–burned cheeks worked itself into my eyes. "See you next year, Grandma!" I told her through tears. "And it will be even better!"

*E*very year is better!" she whispered into my hair, black as crows, like hers used to be. Through the train window, I took this picture of Grandma on the platform, waving, her acorn-diamond ring sparkling a good-bye.

Every year was better for years and years.

And last year, when I woke up at Grandma's house, I took her for a stroll in her wheelchair. I walked her through the paths in the woods, and around the gopher holes in the field. I brought her to the water's edge so that she could feel the pulse of waves on her feet. We rode between the garden rows, picking the greens we needed, and overflowing her lap with firm, fresh flowers.

And even though I collected for the scrapbook all summer long, there were still a lot of blank pages left when Grandma died.

Grandma started that scrapbook because I was once too young to remember, and because one day, I may get too old to remember. My Grandma's gone this year, but somehow she remains, keeping me from forgetting. And sometimes, when I'm all by myself and dreaming of the sea, I can almost feel her right here beside me, filling in the blank pages of my life, her sparkling ring glinting off my hair, black as crows. Like hers used to be.